# In Loving Memory

# Tracey Dominy
## (Mum)

14/10/1963 - 20/08/2022

I love and miss you so much every single day!

Rest peacefully and stay amused at the angel high tea party.

# Contents Page

Page 4: Chapter 1 - Spanish Summer
Page 15: Chapter 2 - Spongy Floor
Page 29: Chapter 3 - 2A

Page 38: Chapter 4 - Uma
Page 44: Chapter 5 - Sas
Page 53: Chapter 6 - Conjuring

Page 68: Chapter 7 - Cartoonevenchenso Station
Page 74: Chapter 8 - Bangles
Page 84: Chapter 9 - Frequency

Page 90: Chapter 10 - Jairaj
Page 100: Chapter 11 - Chip
Page 106: Chapter 12 - Transfer

Page 113: Chapter 13 - Cerne

# Lar Lar Land

## Cartoonevenchenso

## Part 1

### Created by Si Baker

All Rights Reserved©
Copyright 2024©
Completely lar lar publishing©

# Chapter 1: Spanish Summer

Dave and Debbie Lardell walk out of the front door to their somewhat new home moments after getting attacked. Their home has taken a battering, and some parts have been heavily blown up.

Dave, who's completely out of breath, looks at his wife lovingly, knowing that she's safe and alive. "It's been a while since we've had to do that merry-go-round."

Debbie looks at Dave, pulls him closer and gives him a huge kiss. Afterwards, she moves her hand to his left cheek. And calls out loudly, "**OAKLEY!**" The earth around their feet began to move and shake as rumbles from the ground increased in loudness. A huge oak tree walked from behind the house and came towards Debbie and Dave.

It stands there and waits in front of them. Debbie looks at Oakley and tells him, "We need to leave now; you know where to send us."

Oakley bends down only slightly and picks up Debbie and then Dave with its branches; Oakley swings around and sends them towards the sky in opposite directions to each other. Once they're a few thousand feet in the air, a portal opens for them both, and they disappear through it.

# House of Commons, England

The Prime Minister is announcing a new law he's putting through today live to the media from the House of Commons. "I'm delighted to announce today a new law has been passed. A law which to many has been overdue, from this day forward the word *imagination* is banned from use in England.

It's become very apparent that the word makes people who can't use their imagination feel disabled, unequal, separated, depressed, and even suicidal. The rates of suicides have increased significantly over the last twelve months, and this is all unequivocally because of imagination."

The Prime Minister catches his breath before going on to continue, "So now, I'm pleased to say from this day forward, imagination is just a thought. Anyone who is caught using the word will be prosecuted to the full extent of the law, with the possibility of facing life in prison."

The MPs in the House of Commons cheer this news as the Prime Minister takes his seat. Whilst a few are hesitant to get involved with the cheers - they can see that this is starting to send a bad precedent.

Meanwhile, away from the Commons, a huge amount of people watch their TV sets, mobiles and other digital devices with horror. They can't believe what is happening, yet there is also a vast amount that is not surprised at the actions that have been taken by the Prime Minister.

Some have felt there could be a change in the air, the Prime Minister has shown signs of erratic behaviour more and more recently, and he's been searching for and using minuscule reasons to warrant more control.

Saskia is reading the news on her mobile as she walks through the carriage of a train heading towards Maiden Newton. She sits down on a chair that has a table with seats on the other side. Saskia sits down, mumbling to herself. "He can't do this; he's not right in the skull!" Saskia huffs to herself as the train carriage begins to shake more than a train carriage usually would.

Saskia looks around to see if anyone heard her mumble to herself - kind of hoping someone did hear her and that they're in close proximity. Saskia wants to know if they've heard the news also, as she's got some fire in her belly now and wants to have a rant and say her piece.

After looking around, there was nobody close and nobody on the same carriage either. Saskia leans back into her chair fully and looks closer at the two chairs on the other side of the table, "What the heck?"

The chairs are starting to transform into different versions of themselves, almost cartoon-like. The windows to the side of her are doing the same. And then the chair she's sitting on starts following suit.

The chairs opposite her now have faces appearing on them, smiling and singing. "*Trains, trains go by, so clickity in a Spanish summer when sangria wants to take you for a drive. Yet not to matter how it tries to do it, splendour can only be defined by your laugh. So trains, trains go by."*

Saskia gets up as the chairs sing and rock side to side. The whole carriage has changed into an enchanted one full of vibrant cartoon parts singing and talking to itself. Saskia looks all around her and then towards the window to the carriage. When she did, the penny started to drop in her mind. It appears that she's no longer on the normal route to Maiden Newton that she's used to taking. "Oh my!"

This is not her usual route at all.

# Bristol

Hemly is in his home watching the news as he's holding a box of opened washing powder. Hemly has a home with a lounge and open kitchen within the same room. Hemly is in the midst of doing some household chores and is about to put some washing powder into the slot of his washing machine to wash his dirty work clothes that have been mounting up over the course of the week.

Hemly takes another look at his TV screen and steps towards the washing machine. As he begins to look where he's pouring the washing powder, his head and body get sucked completely in.

The powder tray closes, and the washing machine begins to turn on and swiftly transforms into an enchanted, cartoon version of itself. A much smaller version of Hemly appears shortly after in the drum of the washing machine, along with his clothes; moments later, he spins away.

# Thornhill, Southampton

Juanita is walking from her car to get a parking ticket for parking her car in the car park. Juanita walks up to the ticket machine and looks at the sign next to it, which states the prices for a short stay up until a long stay. Juanita only wants to use it for a couple of hours. The price says £1.50, so Juanita looks in her purse and pulls out some change.

Jaunita begins to put some money into the ticket machine, starting with a twenty-pence coin. Followed up with another twenty-pence, a ten-pence, and then lastly, a one-pound coin. As the one pound goes in, so does Jaunita's hand and the rest of her body through the coin slot.

Instantly after the button to pay for the ticket is pressed automatically, the ticket begins to get printed. Once it's finished, out pops a ticket with large lettering printed upon it saying, '*Lar Lar Land*.'

The ticket falls out onto the floor below. When it hits the floor, the ticket starts to move and shapeshift.

# Chapter 2: Spongy Floor

In a bluebell forest walks a man foraging and collecting mushrooms. As he picks up the mushrooms, he puts them into his wicker basket. Appearance wise, the man looks close to seventy years old. He has a white twizzled moustache, a dirty white vest, and some black short-shorts, with nothing on his feet, whilst holding a green rucksack on his back.

As he collects the mushrooms, animals seem to walk, crawl and run towards him rather than away from him. As the foraging man continues to walk, he sings a little song to himself from time to time. "***Bluebells, snowdrops, and mushrooms. Live on the spongy floor, for I can see them following their path once the pores have risen to their adorers. The fungi - the*** *smell, the connection to the other side, the frequency, can change the spell."*

The foraging man walks on, picking up more mushrooms. As he sings, some of the petals from the bluebells start to become enchanted, and they pull themselves off their stems. They start to walk away using their petal parts as feet and hands. They climb down onto the floor and continue to move to the rhythm of the foraging man's song and towards the man himself.

The foraging man sings the same song again *"Bluebells, snowdrops, and mushrooms. Live on the spongy floor, for I can see them following their path once the pores have risen to their adorers. The fungi - the smell, the connection to the other side, the frequency, can change the spell."*

The man takes out a bell from the pocket of his shorts and looks around at the forest. He chimes with the nail from his right index finger, which creates a new frequency. Suddenly all around the forest, everything has changed. Out of nowhere, new things and creatures can be seen everywhere. The foraging man takes a mushroom from his wicker basket and puts one into his mouth with a huge grin on his face.

He walks on chewing the mushroom, and the foraging man begins to pick a fruit from the ground that looks like it's from another dimension or otherworldly. The fruit is multiple colours, gloopy, and rests upon a claw-like foot that has vents to breathe and hum a mystical sound.

The foraging man pulls at the claw-like part to break it away from the ground it's rooted to. As the forager pulls it, the humming sound from the fruit reaches a different pitch. And with a large yank, the foraging man pulls the fruit away from the ground, sending himself backwards, landing on his bottom. "Got ya!"

The forager holds the fruit, and underneath it, the fruit is holding a cubed box, which glows luminescent colours and shades. "Whale tookie-syoki." Comments the man, and the claw part releases the box, and the man using his left hand, takes it. He puts the fruit onto the floor and starts taking his rucksack off his back. He opens the zip to his bag and puts the box in his bag as the fruit walks over to the hole it was pulled out of.

He fastens the zip back up and puts his arms through the handles of his rucksack so it's on his back again. After taking a moment to rub his nose, he gets back onto his feet again. The forager chooses to walk west for three minutes, singing this song from time to time. "*Bluebells, snowdrops, and mushrooms. Live on the spongy floor, for I can see them following their path once the pores have risen to their adorers. The fungi - the smell, the connection to the other side, the frequency, can change the spell.*"

After three minutes, he stops in front of a plant that has a huge tongue licking its only eyeball. The plant stops licking its eye and instead chooses to look at the forager. As he stops, his huge tongue hits the ground with a thud.

The forager pulls out his bell again from his pocket, and this time instead of using his index finger, he uses the nail of his left pinky-finger to tap the bell. When the bell is tapped, a large pitched noise is given off. This noise changes the frequency of the area around him and sends the foraging man into a new environment.

# The Completely Lar Lar Academy of Imagination

Arthur is sitting on the balcony that extends inside his bedroom at the Completely Lar Lar Academy of Imagination. He's got his legs dangling over the wall holding a fishing rod in his hands. Below him is a huge lake filled with chocolate-flavoured fish as well as other surprise species.

Arthur stays there peacefully, soaking in the morning rays from the sky. Around a minute later, Arthur's doorman brings Jerry Stopforth onto the balcony with him. As Jerry arrives and smiles, Arthur gets a huge yank on his fishing rod, and the line begins to tighten as the tip of the rod bends over.

Arthur pulls the rod up and starts reeling in, not overly fast but at the right pace to hook the fish properly and to start bringing it in. The fish struggles against the line and continues to try and swim away. Jerry starts to move toward the balcony, and she climbs up to sit on it next to Arthur.

Jerry watches Arthur as he battles the fish, each time Arthur makes up some ground on the line, the fish then takes it away and swims even further away than where it was before. The doorman walks away and leaves the two on the balcony.

Arthur looks at Jerry and then smiles at her, and then looks back down at the lake. For seven more minutes, Arthur and the fish battled, but Arthur has finally managed to tire the fish out enough, and now it's dangling in the air up towards the balcony.

Arthur stands up and jumps onto the floor of the balcony and then continues to reel in the fish. When the fish arrives at the top and onto the wall of the balcony, Jerry helps pull the thirty-pound fish over the wall and onto the floor where Arthur stands. "Looks like I've arrived at the right time, Arthur."

"Breakfast is ready, Jerry." Arthur's smile couldn't be brighter at the thought of eating this fish.

Five minutes later, the two are sitting on the balcony again. They're holding a plate of chocolate fish whilst looking at the picturesque view in front of them. "I ended up making one of these in my room also."

Arthur looks at Jerry. "Made what?"

"A balcony." Jerry doesn't look at Arthur; she just looks out at the view and at a strange creature swooping down, trying to catch itself a fish from the lake.

"You made a balcony?!" Arthur smiles at her proudly.

"How could I not? I mean - look at what you wake up to every morning! It's literally insane; obviously, the view is totally different. Plus, don't worry, I'll still be coming to yours for breakfast in the morning. I'm still completely crap at fishing!"

Arthur nods his head. "You don't have to agree with me, Arthur."

"But you are crap, Jerry  And I mean that in the politest sense possible."

24

Jerry looks at him and pretends to be jokingly offended. "Oh, really, you're going there?"

"You went there first. I mean, we've only been fishing here for like, I dunno six months, and you caught nothing."

"Gimme that fishing rod, Arthur." Jerry is keen to make a point that she can, in fact, catch a fish.

Arthur looks at Jerry and then looks at the fishing rod and passes it to her. "Here you go, but just remember, mind, we've gotta get to a lesson in twenty minutes."

Jerry moves her breakfast plate out the way and takes the rod. "I'll give you twenty minutes."

Arthur chuckles to himself, "Steady."

Jerry holds the rod firmly in her hands; she moves the catch over on the reel and moves the rod back to then start casting the rod into the lake. After casting the rod successfully near some honeycomb lily pads, they sit and wait. "That was a decent cast, Jerry."

"I know, right." Jerry looks like she's in the zone and gets comfortable.

Ten minutes later, Jerry's face is elated; she can't believe she's actually reeling in her first ever fish! The size of it has to be bigger than forty pounds. Unfortunately, Jerry's celebrations are quickly cut short when a huge creature fly's down and takes the fish and the line with it also. Not only that, Jerry is taken with her rod as she didn't let go in time after being dragged over the balcony.

As it stands now, it's far too late to let go; otherwise, she'll fall completely to the bottom and into the lake. So instead, Jerry is flying through the air, holding onto a fishing rod that's caught a fish that has been caught by a flying creature that's completely made up with Arthur's imagination. "ARTHUR, HELP!" Screams Jerry as she's being whisked away.

Arthur looks over the balcony in horror. "Well, this is unusual circumstances. HANG ON, JERRY!" Arthur is watching Jerry move around all over the place.

Arthur's doorman rushes out onto the balcony. "Well, would you look at that, she caught a fish!"

Arthur is just as surprised. "I never thought she'd catch two things in the same morning."

"Such is life, Arthur, such is life. Shall I go and get her?"

"If you could."

"Very good, sir." Arthur's doorman jumps off the balcony without another moment to hesitate or think.

# Chapter 3: 2A

Underground in the tunnels of Charlton Down walks a man who's six-feet tall, wearing a flat cap. The tunnels were used once upon a time to transport people from mental institutions to prisons and courthouses. For the last thirty years, they've been unused; some would strongly go on to state that they've never been in use.

On the walls to the left of the man, an umbrella appears from out of them. The umbrella fully extends and spins, and seconds later, a woman appears wearing a long grey coat that goes past her knees. As well as a long grey skirt and black boots with laces tied around the top of the boots, twice around.

It's the same woman who picked up that same umbrella from 2A Withall Street. The woman is almost in sync with the man as he walks through the tunnel. She continues to walk with him as he greets her, "Hello, Vioyint."

"Ankori," says Vioyint as she continues to walk. They walk down the tunnel without saying anything for around half a mile, leaving them somewhere between Charminster and Charlton Down.

Once they reach this area, a crystal floats out of the coat of the woman, and it appears in front of them, levitating head height with them. The two of them stand side by side with each other, and they nod to signal they're ready for what is coming next.

The crystal then taps the left of the wall; then it floats over to the right, then it comes central in front of the two again. Then the crystal taps the top (roof of the tunnel) and then to the floor. Once the floor is tapped, the floor crumbles - creating a hole underneath Vioyint and Ankori.

The two fall along with the crystal that starts to fly back into the pocket of Vioyint's coat. The two begin to open their umbrellas as the hole in the tunnel begins to fill back up to how it was previously. As the umbrellas open, the bricks from the tunnel go back upwards along with anything else it had with it previously, like dust and cement.

The two float down into what looks like gold rings surrounded by clouds. There are many of these rings, large enough for umbrellas to fit through. Vioyint goes towards one quite far away from where Ankori is going. Yet both of them pick a ring, and they float down through it. As they go lower, the clouds begin to disappear, and a marble courtroom appears below them. The room doesn't quite look as serious as the standard courtroom we come to know. It looked less serious, less boring, and much more vibrant and imaginative.

The room had many types of beings in there. Some from this dimension, and many who were not, yet they all came here carrying umbrellas. Vioyint and Ankori are one of the last to arrive as the seats they're falling into appear to be some of the last not occupied.

The seats are not fixed to the floor; they're floating, so the seats meet their slow fall. As Vioyint takes her chair, she's greeted by the beings next to her on either side.

Within five minutes, the chairs in the room are full. When the last chair is full, a fireplace in the background lights green, and when it does so, a woman by the name of Wrinous Derkin speaks. "Overseers - do we know why we're all here today?"

The beings in the room in sync reply, "*Indeed*, we do."

Wrinous goes on to ask, "First, I will start by asking for some intelligence from Vioyint on the matter before I ask further questions from the room."

Wrinous shuffles forward in her chair. "Vioyint, do you have any information on how this came to be? And do we know who got through the cracks to influence this matter?"

Vioyint looks at her with some level of confidence. "It looks like from a source that it could be someone with Pai's group. To give a name at this stage would be unwise of me. More time is needed before the person or persons are unveiled."

Wrinous looks at her sternly. "Do you have a short or a vast list of who you're narrowing it down to?"

"Short." Vioyint continues to sit upright.

Wrinous is somewhat pleased with that reply. "And do you think it could be Pai as the perpetrator?"

"At this stage, I don't believe it is Pai herself. Yet more likely someone acting on her behalf or to make it look so."

Wrinous addresses the room with a sad expression, "We know where the next logical step to this leads, don't we? There is only going to be one outcome that now this has been enforced. I will now ask the room, do we have a rough estimate of how long we have until the next stage is enforced?"

Ankori waits to see if anyone else speaks, and nobody is doing so, so he gives his estimate. "Logically within six months. Most likely sooner, when tenterhooks like this are put in place, all we are looking at is one big reason or an orchestrated reason for the next step to happen. So I think we're actually closer to within a month."

The whites of Wrinous's eyes become bigger, "A month?"

Ankori crunches up his face, "I would say so. *Unfortunately*, any longer would be borrowed time."

"Okay, thank you, Ankori. I look to the room now and ask for patience over this time, but not too much. What will be coming is something that can be dealt with, but it's going to be very delicate and very fluid. There are a number of ways we can play this; one is to accept it, see it, experience and tackle it once it hits. The next is prevention, or another is complete and utter retaliation."

Wrinous takes a sip of her drink to help her speaking voice before going on to add. "As this room is one of equals, and my word is not the one that dictates what is to happen next. So as always, I will ask the room - how do you want to play this?"

# Chapter 4: Uma

In a dead land forest appears a girl (9) who is in her jeans, hoodie and ruffed-up trainers. Her hoodie has badges on it from her favourite gothic style bands.

She lays there in the mud on her knees, unsure as to where she is. As she stays there, she looks up, and an animal skull head the size of a building stands there in front of her. Around the forehead area of the skull is a large symbol that looks and acts like the brain tissue. On top of that and surrounding it is a globed dome which has altering images and patterns. The mouth of it is covered with a peculiar creature. The nose hole leaks dark matter, which trails off to the sides and kills what is dead already.

The girl stays there, unsure what to do. She feels that if she's here, then someone would know why. She's not sure if moving right now is the best thing to do. Any ordinary person would look around at where they are, get frightened, panic, run away, and get themselves even more lost but in the hope eventually they would find a way to feel/get safe again.

Instead, this girl decides to sit comfortably crossed-legged in front of the skull and watch it with a smile. As she looks closer, she looks more intently, almost feeling the energy of the destruction that spills out of the mouth of the skull. This seems to energise the girl, the thought that whatever touches it will die. This makes her feel more safe than any fairytale.

# Manchester

A girl called Uma, who's no older than eight, is sitting watching The Addams Family on the family TV in the lounge. She's only watching it as she's listening to some music on her family iPad at the same time. She's sitting on a green sofa as her parents are cooking in the kitchen in the next room.

As Lurch comes into the hallway, the TV flashes and the Munsters can no longer be seen. Instead, the TV stays black and white, and a symbol appears on the screen. The symbol spins slowly; as this happens, the girl's mum starts to run into the room frightfully scared, followed by Uma's dad, who's got pure anger and hatred on his face. Her dad grabs Uma's mum and throws her to the floor. And starts to punch her repeatedly in the face.

He starts to strangle her as Uma's mum looks towards Uma holding her arm out to her daughter, but then has to try and use her arms to stop being strangled.

Uma can't believe what is happening, and she gets up on the sofa, and she starts to panic and cry. The headphone lead from the iPad gets pulled out. Uma can now hear the struggle from her mum, and she can hear her own screams. Her dad looks at her, "Shut up, Uma! Your mum is a filthy bitch!"

Uma looks to the side of the sofa, and there's a side plate with a cheese knife; her dad had cheese and biscuits for lunch earlier. Pure instinct drove her to grab the knife and jump off the sofa towards her father's throat. She stabbed him in the windpipe, and then the next moment, she opened her eyes.

Uma is sitting on her knees in front of a huge skull head the size of a building leaking dark matter. Uma looks at her hand, and she can no longer see or feel a knife in her hand. She can't see her mum, and she can't see her dad or the home she was previously in.

Uma looks to the side, and she sees another girl near her. The girl looks toward her, and her eyes change colour as she looks at her. They turn darkened purple, and once they do, the girl stops looking at her. Instead, she looks toward the skull, and then the girl clenches her fist and starts engraving a shape in the mud in front of where she sits.

The girl engraves a large question mark, and once she does, a symbol appears next to it. A symbol of a hand symbolising 'wait'. The symbol floats out of the ground in front of her face and stays there. Uma looks at the skull and then begins to get fixated.

# Chapter 5: Sas

Saskia gets off the train and onto the platform of a place that is completely perturbing her. "What the?!" She looks around, and everything is animated. Saskia looks at her hands. "They look normal," and then she looks back at the platform and her surroundings. She looked behind her, and the place was crazy. It had cartoon characters walking, running around, selling things, and entertaining passers-by.

Saskia looks behind her and back at the carriage, and now a group of cartoon characters are trying to rob the train as others walk onto the carriages without a care in the world. She begins to walk forwards at a quicker pace trying to make sense of it all. As she does, a jaguarundi walking on two feet (wearing disco pants) bumps into Saskia as he's on a telephone which appears to be a bottle of air freshener. As he talks, he holds the button that releases a spray.

As they bump into each other, the jaguarundi speaks up, "Watch it, kid!" and walks on, speaking into the air freshener. "And when I woke up, the next thing I was melting like a panther holding a lettuce. No, there wasn't soy sauce."

As Saskia looks back, she can't get her head around what just happened, she frowns. A band begins to play music on the platform as crazy cartoon madness seems to arrive at every angle; it's probably the most disorganised business she's ever seen.

Saskia makes her way toward the ticket office. Once she pushes the door open and walks in there, it's like the darkest, chilliest, unwelcomingly lonely ticket office you could imagine. Worse than what you would find at a subway station at three in the morning in the city.

It was almost like she walked into a vortex. The platform was full of life and creatures. In here, it's just her and a two-dimensional woman with blue hair sitting behind a ticket booth on the other side of the room.

As she walked, a chilling gust of wind blew around her ankles, and her footsteps appeared to get louder than what they were before. Saskia wanted to speak to the woman to find out where and why she was there. She looked around at the room, and it still all appeared like something out of a cartoon. As she walked towards the ticket booth, the ticket booth seemed to get further away again with each step. And her footsteps got louder.

As Saskia walked, she thought someone was trying to walk past her as the steps got louder. Saskia looked behind to see if she needed to maybe move out the way to make room, but nobody was coming.

Saskia looked ahead again and started walking towards the booth, yet it seemed that no matter how much she was walking, she wasn't making any distance up. As well as that, the footsteps were getting alarmingly loud. Saskia stopped walking, and the footsteps stopped. When she walked again next, the sound of the footsteps sounded like they had been replaced with ones of an elephant.

The ticket booth was getting even further away. Saskia started running towards the booth, and the noise of the steps was making the ground shake and the walls move, yet the woman in the ticket booth didn't even look up. She just files her nails in her own little world, waiting for someone to turn up at some point and serve.

Saskia stops as she notices that she's getting nowhere quick, and nothing is making sense. She takes a breath, and another, then looks around to see if anyone else is seeing what is happening right now, and nobody else is in the room apart from her and the lady behind the desk.

Saskia has a new idea; she begins to start walking again, but this time on tiptoes and ever-so quiet. She thinks that possibly if she does this, she can sneak up on the booth. As she does this, it makes an even louder noise and actually makes the walls to the side crack and split. This dumbfounded Saskia, so instead, she walks back on herself the way she came, and this comes easy. The door she walked through was not trying to move away from her.

This gives her some level of confidence, knowing she's not completely trapped in a room. Saskia tries to walk back towards the booth, and it begins to move away. Saskia then tries something she hasn't tried just yet, "**Um, excuse me, could I have some help, please**?"

The ticket booth woman looks up and stops doing what she's doing. She looks toward the girl and pushes a button, and talks into a microphone which echoes through the speakers in the room, "Did you call for assistance?"

Saskia nods her head and agrees, "Yes - yes, please." As she says this, the booth on the other side of the room, along with the wall it's attached to, starts to move towards Saskia. So much so that by the time it's done moving, it's actually only half a metre away from where Saskia is standing. Once it's stopped moving, the woman behind the ticket booth looks at Saskia.

The two just stare at each other for an over prolonged time before the woman goes on to enquire, "Well - what do I do you for?"

Saskia isn't sure where to start, "Um, I was wondering why I was here?" The woman's eyelids appear to go heavy; once they do, she points to the side of her, which has a sticker attached to the window saying '*NO PHILOSOPHICAL LIFE QUESTIONS ABOUT LIFE*.'

This wasn't a sign that Saskia had previously seen, and it's a sign she certainly didn't expect to be pointed to. "Oh, okay, let me try and rephrase that a different way. I'm lost."

The woman behind the booth points to the sign again. Saskia has to think for a moment as to why she has done that.

Saskia goes on to explain, " I don't mean in life, I mean this is not the platform I wanted to get off on when I got my train ride. I was wondering if you could tell me where I am location wise? Like where the heck is this place in the world, and how I got here? I wanted to be in Maiden Newton."

The woman looks at Saskia deadpan in the face and waits for a moment before going to say, "Well, sure you're here in Cartoonvevenchenso, and the likelihood is you were brought here to die. Have a good day now, chow-chow then." The woman then grabs a shutter blind and pulls it down from the top of the glass. Saskia can no longer see the woman.

"Cartoonvevenchenso?" Saskia says to herself.

# Chapter 6: Conjuring

Arthur is doing a class lesson at the academy in a room that he's not been in before. The person giving the class is Ms Wondrous Wonderment; she's not given this type of lesson to the children. Everything they learn is always a new tool in a slow progression to the next thing.

The room they're standing in is very large, full of encryptions on the walls of languages that don't look earthly. But in the middle of it is a huge ancient symbol on the floor. The children stood around that symbol with a large distance between each person.

Ms Wondrous Wonderment looks at the children, who include Jerry, Arthur, Tegan, and Jan. "This room I've brought you to today is very special and sacred. You should all be honoured to be here. Within here is the next step in your development when it comes to building and creating imagination."

"So it's not a devil-worshipping room?" Cheekily remarks Tegan.

"It could be; it's not what we're using it for, though. At this moment in time, you've been taught how to create new imaginative ideas and store them for others. Is that correct?" The group nodded in agreement, "And how was that?"

Arthur answers first, "Weird and not easy."

Followed by Jan, "The first time I brought imagination out myself for storage, I physically shat myself."

Tegan looks at Ms Wondrous, "There might have been a little poop."

Jerry responds, "Free of poop."

"Okay, so far, you've learned how to create imagination on your own and shit your pants, but have you learned how to create something new together? What this lesson is going to do is put emphasis on that aspect of it. This symbol you are standing around is going to bind or, for a better word, conjoin what you each create together and keep it there safely. And if it's worth keeping, we'll store it. Think of it as a bit of a Ghostbusters trap, but we call it the conjuring conjoiner."

"The conjuring conjoiner?" said Arthur to himself under his breath.

"The conjuring conjoiner works like this - after you conjure and bring the imagination out of your body, it gets placed within, let's say, an energy field. Or better known to us as the conjuring conjoiner. It holds it there and moulds it together in the safest way possible whilst the process happens and continues to do so until it's put in a unit.

And then the next process happens. Essentially what you're doing is taking one thing from one place and putting it in another in the safest way possible.

What I'll ask you all to do is individually create something, but it will be a part of something. For instance, like a head, then the other would pick an arm or an ability, and eventually, we'll stick it all together."

Ms Wondrous looks at them seriously for a moment, "There is an element of safety needed to be involved here, like the Ghostbusters. If you cross the streams the wrong way, it can be a lot harder for the conjoiner to make it stick. What I'm trying to get at is, look at the team around you, know them.

If they think of something, try to make the next thing blend with it and make it follow suit. Use your imagination again if you need to, to think of something new to complement your teammate.

Sure your idea might be individually brilliant on its own, but does it hinder the team as a collective? Always look for the most positive solution to a problem."

Ms Wondrous Wonderment goes on to add, "I would like the group to come up with a new idea for a superhero. The superhero is to be a cartoon character."

"A superhero cartoon character?" Excitedly asked Jan.

Ms Wonderous Wonderment nods, "That's right?"

"Man, I love superheroes! Especially Spiderman," said Tegan.

"Well, that's the type of thing I'm looking for. Do you know how much that spiderperson has influenced people - given them hope? It will exceed a far greater number than you would expect. And the ones that do really well can even provide people with jobs, give them a better life. The knock-on effect can be incredible. I bet between you, somewhere at home, you've got some merchandise!"

"Damn straight," Jan stated.

"Shall we give it a go then?" Ms Wondrous looked at the individuals in the group to see if they were all on board and knew what they were doing. It's a lot to take in within a short space of time.

Jerry looked like she had an idea that she wanted to say before they started. "How good would it be if we came up with a superhero together and we did it for somebody who was homeless? Though the best bit is they ended up having their own superhero movie, and they made millions of pounds and could have lots of homes and sweets."

As Jerry finishes talking, Jopanoodle Lady Dar walks into the room and up to Ms Wondrous Wonderment. She jumps up to the same height as her ear and whispers in it. Jopanoodle floats in the air as long as she needs to, to finish saying what she needs to say. Once she has finished doing that, she floats slowly to the floor again and then starts to walk out of the room, but before she does, she just disappears instead.

Jan clearly liked the idea. "That would be great. Can we do that, Ms Wondrous Wonderment?"

"This is possible, I've been made aware of someone we could do this for, but I must stress you're possibly slightly overconfident. And I stress, possibly - remember you've never actually used the conjuring conjoiner before! And you've never done this together."

Ms Wondrous Wonderment refrains from patronising them before they've given it a good crack, yet wants them to realise this is a serious thing and it's not as simple as just turning up.

"This is not an easy thing to do - so many have failed on their first day doing this. The key is flowing off each other as a group, being humble and adapting."

Ms Wondrous feels like she's given enough fair warnings, and they're ready to start having a go. "Shall we give it a go?"

The children nod at her, and they nod in excitement. Ms Wondrous goes on to ask the group what she'd like "What I'd like you to do is come up with different character traits between yourselves. Hopefully, after you can bring those traits to the conjuring conjoiner here in the room, it will bring together quite the hero at the end of it."

"I'll start you off with a little rhyme - *You can co, you can con, you can conjoin-er. With the conjuring conjoiner. So use your imagination and see what it has to say. Can you co-conjoin a superhero within a learning day? What does it look like? What is its power? Does its farts only travel twenty miles an hour?"*

Ms Wondrous looks toward Jerry to see what she can do. Jerry has her eyes closed; she seems focused and starts looking within herself to see what she wants to draw out. "I want one who helps the homeless with its power." Jerry focuses her mind, and the energy starts to come out of her body. Jerry opens her eyes, and she can gracefully see her energy begin to move towards the conjuring conjoiner, the energy floats above the ancient symbol.

Jan is looking fascinated at the energy Jerry has brought out of her body. Jan knows it's his turn, so he shut his eyes and started focusing on something that might be helpful. Jan thinks of something "Or one who's ultra-wealthy." Jan focuses his mind stronger and can feel his muscles spasm slightly up his back. This energy he creates starts to come out of his body.

The energy comes out in fits and bursts in a green, gold and silver type colour and heads towards the conjuring conjoiner. The energy starts circling around the energy that Jerry created and begins to find a way to mould. Jan opens his eyes and is excited to see another energy surround the one that Jerry has done.

Tegan, without needing to wait any longer, shut her eyes and instantly said, "Who can teleport no matter how tall the tower."

Tegan focuses her mind, and the energy starts to come out of Tegan and to move towards the conjuring conjoiner. The other two energies that Jerry and Jan created start moving toward Tegan's.

The energies seem to respond kindly to each other. Arthur notices this, and it's his turn. He concentrates and focuses on his breathing. Arthur thinks of something which could help it blend smoothly together. "She should be tall." He focuses his mind, and the energy starts to come out of Arthur and trickle towards the conjuring conjoiner. The energy towers above the other, and they decide to join underneath it.

Tegan has her eyes closed; she has already thought of something and decides to add another feature and goes on to add, "And tough." She focuses her mind, and the energy starts to come out of Tegan's body towards the conjuring conjoiner.

Jan wants this ability for the hero "And say's when *enough* is *enough*!" The energy starts to come out of his body, almost flexing-steadily towards the conjuring conjoiner.

A superhero begins to come alive with a conjuring conjoiner; it floats within the ancient symbol. As it does, Ms Wondrous Wonderment focuses on the hero and makes sure it is done safely, with love, and created for the right reasons.

Ms Wondrous Wonderment begins to chant, ***"Hold these traits in the conjuring conjoiner; you do this with love with the*** *hope of transform-e-er. To change people's lives with pure imagination, no matter the frequency, it's pure and will be stationed."*

The children stand looking at the hero as Ms Wondrous Wonderment chants the words again. Ms Wondrous Wonderment begins to chant, *"Hold these traits in the conjuring conjoiner; you do this with love with the hope of transform-e-er. To change people's lives with pure imagination, no matter the frequency, it's pure and will be stationed."*

Ms Wonderous makes sure everything is running smoothly. She looks at the children as they continue to look at the hero floating. As it floats, it starts to transform into an energy in the shape of the ancient symbol and then from time to time into other energetic shapes.

*"You'll stay encapsulated until your day of delivery; that's when the mind's eye will see."*

The floor underneath the symbol begins to open with a fluorescent light bellowing out. The hole opens up big enough for the energy of the hero to move downwards into. Bit by bit, the energy is being drawn downwards. It wasn't trying to do it aggressively; everything was calm. The children step backwards slightly more and watch what they created move on to the next phase.

## Chapter 7 – Cartoonevenchenso Station

Saskia is still standing in the ticket office at Cartoonevenchenso Station, trying to get her head around being in Cartoonevenchenso. And being told that she has probably been brought here to die.

Saskia looks at the shutter and then looks back towards the door and starts to turn and walk towards it. Before she can get there, the shutter opens again, and the woman speaks into the microphone. "Are you Saskia?"

Saskia turns around and is happy to hear her name being mentioned, "Yeah - I'm Saskia." Saskia walks towards the counter, but the counter moves towards her again.

The woman speaks through the microphone, "Sorry I didn't put the dots together; you're one of those human things, aren't you?!"

Saskia agreed, "Yeah, I'm human."

The woman pulls a face of sympathy like she feels sorry for her, "Sorry to hear that. Where you come from, you can't do things like this." The woman prints out a train ticket and slices the top of her head off with it, rips out her brain and lobs it behind her. Within the same motion, she then grabs a can of fizzy drink and shakes it up really hard.

The ticket booth woman opens the can up and pours it into her head. After that, from her jacket, she grabs a drinks umbrella, stabs her eyeball and pulls it out and pops it into the top of her head.

With the usable eye she has, it looks towards a tube. She grabs it, sticks it in her head and uses the other end to drink out of it. The woman rests her elbow on the desk and then puts her chin into her hand and keeps it there. Saskia and the ticket booth woman look at each other as the umbrella slowly moves down, and the woman guzzles her drink. As her eye fixed in her head starts to wonder. "Can you?"

Saskia is stunned at what she is seeing, "No."

The ticket booth woman looks at Saskia and begins to feel even more sorry for her, "Arr - that's a shame. It can really help you cut down on buying crockery."

"It would be nice to buy fewer bowls." Saskia is becoming even more unsure as to what is going on right now.

"Oh, like you wouldn't believe."

Saskia "Sorry, did you say you knew me?"

The ticket booth woman looks at her, "Nope, I have absolutely no idea who you are, I'm afraid." This disappoints Saskia, yet the woman went on to continue, "Yet I did get sent a message saying that someone will be coming to pick you up."

This is a kind of happy surprise for Saskia to hear; as a few moments ago, it seemed like she was getting nowhere quickly. "That's great. Where will I be getting picked up from?"

"Sorry, did I say get picked up?" The ticket booth wondered to herself.

Saskia confirms this, "Yes, that's what you said. Somebody will be coming to pick me up."

"I meant you'll get found at some point. It is always so much easier to relay messages when you've got a brain in your skull. Did I mean relay or rely?" The woman wonders to herself what the actual message is. "Maybe this would be easier with a brain in my head." The woman looks behind to see if her brain is close by, but it's not. She looks back at Saskia, who is waiting patiently, "I'm sure we can muddle through it. Your brain is to be found in Catoonevenchenso."

Saskia is making sure she heard that properly, yet she thinks that maybe she got that wrong also - regarding her brain. Before saying anything, she waits to see if there is any more information.

The ticket booth woman looks at her with her wandering eye and takes another swig of her drink through the tube. "In the meantime, enjoy the sights, and buy some gifts for your friends and family. And cause plenty of trouble."

"Sorry, wait one moment; you expect me to walk out there, and someone will find me."

The ticket booth woman looks at her with a deadpan face and moves her finger to a button. "Uh-huh." The button releases a large spring in the floor that Saskia is standing on, which sends Saskia in the air and through the roof of the building.

# Chapter 8 – Bangles

On a beach in Goa (India) are five children who are trying to sell badges, bracelets, bangles and other things along these lines to tourists. Three of these children (Reyansh, Jairaj and Meera) have been doing this for a couple of years now, whilst the other two (Shyla & Yash) have only been doing this for the last six months.

The children watch two travellers sit down on the beach with their backpacks. They arrived not so long ago after parking their rented motorbikes along the beachfront.

After several minutes the children, one by one, start to make their way over with their merchandise. Once the first child gets there (Reynash), he notices straight away

74

that one of them has got bangles on his wrist. "Hello, hello, where are you from?"

The two men look at the child, and they already notice what is going to happen here. These two guys have been travelling for quite a while, and it's not the first time they've seen someone coming up to them trying to sell them some tourist stuff. It happens all the time in Goa. So without even looking properly at what the child has to offer, Reynash instantly gets dismissed. "Not interested."

Jairaj walks behind Reynash and pushes Reynash out the way to get in front of him. "Are you from England?"

"Yeah!" Replied the other traveller, who was less fed up with getting offered stuff to buy in India.

Jairaj, "Do you know the Queen?"

Before they could answer, Shyla had caught up along with the rest of them. "I know the Queen."

"I know-I know the Queen too." Claimed Yash.

Jairaj, "No, you don't, Yash."

Yash steps from side to side as he tries to get his words out. "I do too. I saw her on TV. She's very old, and her jewels give her neck ache because they're so heavy."

The two travellers start to warm to the little sellers. Meera, the last one to talk, notices that they're starting to lighten up and that's when she starts to try and make her pitch. "Would you like to buy a necklace? Three-hundred rupee? Do you like this one?"

The first traveller who initially said he wasn't interested originally repeats again that he doesn't want anything but in a kinder tone this time. "Nah, sorry, as you can see, I've already got one."

Meera looks at him with a serious face, and then she pulls a cheeky face and then tells the traveller, "Don't be a plonker, Rodney, 'ow about this one?"

The two travellers look at each other and start laughing to themselves; they really didn't expect those words to come out of her mouth, especially Goa.

They look at Meera, "Where did you learn that from?"

Meera looks really pleased with herself, "Only Fools and Horses, on the TV."

The traveller, who is known as Rodney, goes on to compliment Meera. "Well, your cockney accent is very good. Shouldn't you be in a school or something?"

Shyla tells the travellers, "We don't go to school."

Meera looks along with the rest of the children. They would love to go to school. " It's alright, bruv, this is our school."

The travellers chuckled the way she said 'bruv' is not typical of how someone from Goa would usually say it. '"How did you learn English?"

Meera explains, "From TV and the beach. You want to buy a bangle? See you have one like this; you want another?" She holds up her tray of bangles and bracelets.

The traveller looks at his bangles. "Why would I want another if I already have one?"

Meera looks at him with a cheeky grin, yet still disheartened at his response. "Go on, Rodney, two-hundred and fifty rupees, it's a good deal."

The friend of the traveller starts chuckling that Meera keeps calling him Rodney and says, "She's got you on the wire, dude."

Meera starts laughing as she says, "You don't want to be a muppet all your life." Meera's beach friends start laughing between themselves, and the travellers laugh at them laughing.

Rodney, the traveller, now looks at Meera, "So you got all your witty comebacks from TV and the beach, hey?!"

Meera stands proud like Peter Pan, "Uh-huh."

Rodney, the traveller, feels into his short pockets and pulls out seven hundred rupees. Counts it and then gives her six-hundred rupees. "Here you go, keep the bangles for the next person. And go and watch some more TV."

Meera looks really happy as she's handed the money. "Thank you, Rodney." Meera does a little bow and then looks toward the other traveller. "Del, you should be more like your brother. Namaste," Rodney and Del chuckle to themselves as Meera looks at them both cheekily and then skips away happily with her beach friends.

Fifteen minutes later, the children have left the beach, and they start to divide the money. Meera is trying to give them some money, and there's been some bickering between them. Meera has come out of a little shop to get some drinks and fruit. She hands out the drinks and fruit to the youngest first and then finishes with the oldest. Meera goes back to the youngest Shyla & Yash, and Meera gives them fifty rupees each. And then gives Reyansh one-hundred rupees, and then the same to Jairaj.

Jairaj is not happy with what he's been given and feels that he should have more and Meera should have less. Jairaj and Meera are the same age, yet Meera seems to control the group better as she's more organised and she knows how to sell better because she's learnt a vast amount of good sales catchphrases. Plus, she knows how to replenish stock.

Jairaj looks at Meera and explains he wants more; this has started to play on him for quite a while. He feels he should be a more dominant figure and have a bigger say in how things would be separated. Meera knows that if Jairaj was to do this, everything would go wrong within a week. The money they make mostly goes back to their parents and plays an important role in their home life.

The reason these children are not at school is they need to make money and learn how to make money from an early age to help their parents pay the bills and make ends meet.

Jairaj has a moment where his blood begins to boil, and he pushes Meera from the pavement and into the road. Meera doesn't expect this from Jairaj, and she's completely pushed off balance.

Meera stumbles backwards and falls onto the dusty road. She looks back at Jairaj as a rickety local bus with an ancient symbol printed on it hits her. Jairaj opens his eyes.

# Chapter 9: Frequency

In a peculiar world stands a peculiar man carrying a basket of mushrooms and otherworldly flowers. The man has hundreds of creatures following him. As he sings, "**Bluebells, snowdrops, and mushrooms. Live on the spongy floor, for I can see them following their path once the pores have risen to their adorers. The fungi - the smell, the connection to the other side, the frequency, can change the spell.**"

He walks towards a translucent tree with energy, orbs, and static filling it up. The man looks at it, and an orb begins to surround the man. Once it fully surrounds him, he walks toward the tree and into the trunk of it. Once he's in there, he then begins to separate into various different orbs and begins to float in and out of the tree. Some of the orbs stay in the trunk, which also extends into the branches, whilst other orbs move downwards into the roots and ground.

One of the orbs goes into the ground and moves through it like butter. After a period of time, it begins to become larger in size. As it does, it also spins in a supersonic fashion over and over again. Until it stays in one place, just spinning at a pace that can't be recorded by human technology.

The brightness around the ball becomes blinding, and shortly after, the orbs burst into one big electromagnetic pulse. Sending positive shockwaves all through the network of the earth in the ground. Some of the orbs are taken to a new environment in a tranquil area completely separated from the known. All that stays there currently is energy, a flattened ancient stone with encryptions, and a crystal levitating above it.

The area is very still, and as the orbs become brighter, the crystal becomes brighter also. For various minutes the orbs and the crystal appear to almost charge each other up with more energy. Even though, at times, the orb's brightness would change individually, the brightness and sparkle would only increase.

Suddenly the crystal started to spin where it was whilst still levitating. The orbs began to hum a frequency, sparkle and flicker, and this went on again for minutes. Once that was done, the orbs began to circulate around the crystal, charging it up even more than they had been already. The orbs got quicker and direct in their movements, trying to surround the crystal with a coat of energy.

Eventually, the orbs were going so fast with their movements around the crystal you could no longer see the crystal. The only thing you could see of the crystal was rays of brightness coming off from it.

Although this was only momentary as the orbs did surround the crystal entirely as they spun around it at an infallible pace. The orbs were careful to never touch or collide with the ancient stone underneath the crystal as the orbs, and the crystal began to conjoin together as one item.

The orbs circulate the crystal for what could be considered days in time and, to others, infinite. However, there was a moment that came when it stopped. And something new happened, or something similar to what had been known before.

The man who went down the tree was foraging again in an entirely new mystical setting. With items that floated and suspended in the air, except one thing that was fixed upon the floor. The items that were floating in the air were ancient symbols - an excruciating amount of them.

The symbols are otherworldly, dimensional, and the rest in between. To understand these symbols would take up your whole life to understand, and that still wouldn't be enough time either. To understand these symbols, you would have to live numerous lives, and even that would take dedicating all of your time to it.

The chances are that to understand these symbols, you either made them or you lived infinite lives. Some of these symbols are glowing to show that they're in use in a certain dimension. And this is what the man is choosing to look at momentarily. The man walks around for a while, looking at the various symbols in use.

As he looks at the symbols, he shows minimal facial expression; none of this is alarming to him. He walks, looking above and flicking his head only to the ones in use. He doesn't need to stop to understand the meaning of the symbol. He moves like he knows where each symbol is placed.

# Chapter 10: Jairaj

Jairaj opens his eyes, and all around him are young children sitting on the floor not far away from a skull head the size of a building. Jairaj is really freaked out; the last time he had his eyes open, he was watching Meera get hit by a car.

Surely it would be Meera who would be here and not him, he thought to himself internally. For a moment, he wondered to himself whether he had died and not Meera. Otherwise, why would he be here? This clearly isn't Goa!

As he looked around, there was no noise from the children; all of them seemed relatively calm, not panicking or trying to leg it and run away at the nearest opportunity. As he continued to look, he noticed that some of the children had symbols above their heads and in front of them.

Jairaj looked more intently at the skull; he watched the dark matter spill from it. And like other children, he found it captivating, and he watched as everything it touched had no chance of living anymore. Immediately this warmed Jairaj with a sense of familiarity that he'd been struggling to find.

He understood when he looked at the skull that it didn't feel bad for what it was doing, it was not even flinching. And that's how he feels about Meera, she came in his way, and she had to be stopped.

Jairaj started to get an overwhelming feeling to sit more comfortably and began to do so. He sat on his bottom and crossed his legs, and watched the skull. This started to calm him, and he started to fully forget momentarily about what happened to Meera. Or why he's here, he just looked at the skull.

The skull started to change colour, and a purple flash arose above it. The children were no longer in front of the skull; they were underneath it in an eerie room filled with dark magic and energy.

Kaladropi stood there in front of them all, and she waited for the children to get their bearings and calm down with the shock and chit-chatting between themselves. When natural silence came but without it being asked for by Kaladropi. A dark-blue flame appeared shortly, followed by Pai.

When Pai arrived, there was a lot of shock and murmurs from within the room. Not many children have seen something like this happen unless it was on TV. Pai, like Kaladropi, waits for natural silence before Pai addresses the group.

"You are here for one of many reasons; top of the list is because I want you here. After strong recommendations from Kaladropi, who is standing next to me. I want you here, but I hate you, don't take it personally; it's just my makeup. And my makeup says, take it personally as frankly I couldn't give a shit. You're brats, little bastards, and many of you are not even wanted by your parents. I mean, christ, look at ya, some of you have even killed your parents, and you're only a few years out of shitty-smelly diapers.

So my offer to you is, you're going to be trained to shut the fuck up, listen, and stop positive, imaginative thoughts from reaching people. As inside, you're just a bunch of angry little bastards who want things to get destroyed. And we're here to help with that process."

Kaladropi starts to walk around the room, looking at the children and making her presence felt as Pai continues to talk. "As well as this, you'll be trained to create the darkest and most cruel imaginative thoughts for people to act upon. Those are the key points at this stage. The next point is I'm not here to mother you; quite the opposite, I'm the worst possible character you could meet. I'm every type of swear word you can think of."

Alex speaks up, "Can we call you one?" Pai then sends Alex flying in the air towards a wall, and she rips his body apart into pieces without blood falling. He stops just before he hits the wall; the pieces of his body are floating in the air, his head (severed) is looking at Pai, and Alex is still able to blink and listen.

Pai calmly looks at Alex, "Yes, you can, Alex. In fact, if you call me anything heartwarmingly positive, you will die. And that goes for the rest of you rusty succubuses. If you speak to me and your words don't have venom in them, just know that there are no second chances. You won't be speaking out of your mouth anymore. I'll make sure the best you wish for is people wondering if you're talking or farting."

"So I plead to the group to look at Alex and notice right now how fragile his life is. Although he does have a choice, his next words are very important if he wants to continue living. Not for any particular thing he did wrong; it's just because I'm a big old-fashioned twisted psychopath, and I like people feeling threatened by everything I do or say. Anything else would just be, well, polite, wouldn't it?!

Wouldn't it, Alex? Don't worry, I'll answer that for you, Alex. Yes, it would, Pai! And being polite comes from a nice place, a positive place. A place where I want you to **fucking forget about**!" After raising her voice, Pai calms herself and goes on to continue in her own twisted way.

"If I just let him down in one piece, he would probably thank me for saving his life out of pure instinct. It's not his fault; it's his upbringing, it's how most people react when their lives are spared, many are thankful for it instantly." Pai moves around Alex. As she does, darkened crystals begin to float upwards and move around the room in a breathing motion that is in sync with Pai's.

"And if Alex did thank me, well, I would have to kill him straight away, which defies the point of me sparing his life at this point. Now you might be wondering, well, isn't that somewhat nice knowing that he could have said that, so you've stopped that happening already by preempting it?!" Pai screams, "**NO!**"

Pai looks back at the children, but her body doesn't move. Her eyes widened like a psycho. "It's just a fucking lesson, and somehow I had to make my point. And killing him in front of you for no reason whatsoever would be very cliche." Pai looks at Alex. "What do you say, dipshit? I'll let you talk and steal the room now. This is your stage."

Alex looked at her and went on to state with his face scrunched up, "Fuck off and die."

"You're learning." Pai drops all the pieces of Alex to the ground, but before they hit the ground, they all come together. Alex is now back in one piece.

Alex gets up very quickly and scurries away to the rest of the group, hoping that is that. From now Alex will do the utmost to say nothing unless spoken to.

Pai goes on to add without showing any more interest in Alex. "For now, you'll be taken to your quarters where you will receive food and can rest, and then tomorrow, training begins on your fragile-twisted minds. That will be all."

Pai disappears from the room. As she does, numerous more elders arrive in the room to help Kaladropi take the children to where they need to go next.

# Chapter 11: Chip

In a conference room stands a group of medical scientists, engineers and entrepreneurs, as well as a case study on stage in front of an intrigued crowd.

A woman called Kenzie Wiral stands in front of the group, who is the founder of a new microchip called 'The Support-Me-Chip'. The microchip she is discussing via microphone is to rival big companies such as Neuralink.

The chip implanted in the brain is to help medical conditions such as MS, Fibromyalgia, Parkinson's, and a host more. As well as this you'll have access to the internet and a tropic of other uses.

The long-term studies and tests that have been done have been approved for commercial use.

"I would like to thank the team for bringing such an important piece of medical technology to people who need it. This has proved, without doubt, a life-changing moment for so many people. People who've been in care now no longer need to be looked after, people who used to take fifteen minutes to walk down the stairs can now run up them. People with over two hundred types of symptoms like fibromyalgia can now move pain-free.

The Support-Me-Chip has been a revelation to many, but there are still so many that are not even aware of this piece of technology, and that's why we want to get it to the far reaches of the globe as quickly as possible. The more people who can help us reach these people, the better.

Understandably, talking money should be an afterthought, but the money that this can save hospitals and doctor surgeries whilst also minimising waiting lists would be extraordinary. It would be something that hasn't been seen for decades.

On that note, I would like to thank you for your time in coming here today to listen to us and about our project."

The crowd get up from their seats and begin to applaud Kenzie and the rest of the people who are standing on stage who've been talking throughout this conference. Kenzie nods and thanks the crowd with hand gestures as others on stage clap the crowd for their time and participation.

## Four Months Later

The Prime Minister is having a media press conference from Downing Street. "I'm holding this conference today in front of you, the people of England, to make you aware of a new law that has been passed. This law is now in place with immediate effect.

This law will punish anyone for displaying public use of what would have been known prior as positive imagination. Creating things with a positive imagination for positive benefits is now illegal. We're entering a war on a war, a war on crime, whilst people meanwhile are killing themselves as they think this is a positive step. And I'm sure we can all agree that killing yourself is not positive.

This country is in for a rude awakening, we think for you now, and we're at war, and we need thoughts that are there to punish our victims and take their land that is rightfully ours as the greatest country in the world. Supported by the greatest party that's ever been put in place.

I'm proud to say that we've passed more laws than we ever have had under any other Prime Minister." The Prime Minister takes a moment and then goes to further add.

"This is why I'm strengthening this law even further by doing the following." The Prime Minister glances at his notes in front of him and goes on to say, "Anyone who has a Support-Me-Chip is now currently in the process of having an automatic upgrade as this press conference is being held."

The Prime Minister glances at his notes, "This upgrade meets the laws expected of society here in England and will restrict access to that automatic response and use of your brain.

This has been done, so you no longer need to worry about those what-if moments. It will preempt you to stop before you've even started, giving you peace of mind that you'll never get arrested doing so by force of habit.

This is why now the 'Support-Me-Chip' is now available without having to have a medical condition prior. I strongly suggest that anyone who feels that they might need these chips in the times ahead go and get one for themselves or even their loved ones. It could be the chip that keeps you out of prison, and that's obviously the last place we want you to be."

# Chapter 12: Transfer

A year later, after banning public use of positive imagination in England, students at the Completely Lar Lar Academy of Imagination stand in front of Master Baldrick. They're standing in a moving chamber, each getting transferred imaginative thoughts.

These students in front of him are going to be entering a town on Earth to deliver some imaginative thoughts to people. These students are doing this for the first time. The students in front of Master Baldrick are Jerry, Rusty, Jan, Tegan, Nobbo, and Arthur.

Each student is also doubled up with more experienced people, yet their faces are covered with a mask of symbols only revealing their eyes. These are the people transferring the students the imaginative thoughts to pass on again. They're currently transferring it by making the children hold a crystal box.

Once the designated person touches the crystal box, it then moves and transforms almost into a liquid and melts around the hands of the deliverer. As the process begins, it moves all around the arms and body of the person.

Eventually, it seeps into their skin and disappears within them, only to be brought back out later and transferred to its designated person. Master Baldrick looks at the students and waits for every child to get the transfer via the crystal. Rusty is the last one to go through the process by touching the crystal. Rusty tries to calm himself as the process is happening.

"I'm sure I saw this in the Matrix after Morpheus gives Neo a pill and he touches the mirror." Rusty watches his arms as the liquid crystal climbs up his arms towards his shoulders and neck.

This process gives Rusty a chill. "Gee, that's cold. You'd at least expect melted crystal to be warm, right?!" Before it reached his neck, it seeped into his skin and disappeared, which calmed Rusty down.

Master Baldrick waited for Rusty to settle; it's not the first time Master Baldrick has done this. Each child reacts differently to the transfer process and the anxiety about going out to deliver imagination.

Once he's got their full attention, it's only then that he speaks. "Right, remember we are not a bunch of witches on broomsticks throwing potions about like newspaper boys. We are much more delicate than that."

The children are trying not to smirk and stay focused as Master Baldrick continues. "We blend, we use our environment that's around us. We change frequencies when we need to, which will get you out of sight from another person's reality if needed."

Master Baldrick keeps serious as he states, "Do not get seen; that's the ultimate goal here. Pai's army and others are out there, and one of their primary goals is to stop you as best they can from delivering anything.

Anything at all! It can be wild, and this is not going to be how you remember Earth previously. You're now going to see more than you've ever seen. Each person is either getting sent good imagination, bad imagination, or there's a war in between stopping any of it getting anywhere. The last place you want to be is seen in the last place I mentioned.

This is why you're doubling up with an experienced partner whose role is to protect you on your journey. They're here to make sure you get to the end and deliver the imagination to the designated person. The chances are if you weren't doubled up on your first day, you would probably die."

Master Baldrick takes a saddened, deep breath before going on to add, "Actually, we know that's the case as we've tried it with students on their own before. And some have died with their doubles. Also, that's a reason to put your masks on."

The kids are starting to look a little more scared and a little bit more aware of what they're walking into. They put on their masks. "So my biggest suggestion is to stay extra close to your partner, listen to them, they will be your guide. I'll be keeping an eye on all of you.

If at any point you get separated, your double up dies, or you feel this is too much. Make sure that you press and hold the button that's fastened in your jacket pocket."

Master Baldrick is very serious about this and wants to make sure that everyone is listening to him and fully focused. "This will send you automatically to a protected safety spot. You stay there, unless you don't feel safe or that place has been violated or breached. If that happens, you press it again or again until you're in a safe zone.

Once this has happened, a member of the academy will come and collect you and bring you back here."

Master Baldrick looks at the group and asks them kindly, "Any further questions?" The group looks at him, and they look at him without saying anything. "I'll take that as a no. Shall we get going then?"

Before the children had a chance to speak or respond, they had all disappeared from the chamber and the Completely Lar Lar Academy of Imagination to deliver imagination.

# Chapter 13: Cerne

Master Baldrick, Jerry, Rusty, Jan, Tegan, Nobbo, and Arthur are doubled up with another group wearing masks with ancient symbols on them. They arrived in Cerne Abbas (Dorset) within the dead of the night. As soon as they arrive outside the Church, Master Baldrick re-sends them to their partner they're partnering up with to separate parts of Cerne. When you're delivering imagination, you don't want to be seen in large groups, or even at all.

Arthur and his partner are sent outside a white cottage belonging to the Farley family. The cottage was very old and very beautiful, with ivy going up the front of it towards the thatched roof. The person who

Arthur is partnered up with waits to see if the coast is clear but without spending too much time to be potentially seen in the process.

Arthur's partner whispers, "Ivy - now!" He transforms/shapeshifts into a leaf of ivy and blends into the stems. Arthur followed suit, and they did this via different stems all the way up to the top window frame. The two then camouflage themselves as a window frame and then into a glass pane each. They waited to see what/who was in the room and if it was safe to enter.

As they looked into the room, Mr and Mrs Farley were sleeping on their double bed. The room was very still, no lights were turned on, but you could still see quite well as the curtains were left open, and moonlight shone through.

Arthur and his partner were in no hurry to make their move to safety, and getting it to the right person is everything when delivering imagination. After a considerable time waiting, Arthur shapeshifts into the bricks of the walls in the room, moving from one brick into the cement that holds it together, and then onto the next. He does this all the way around the room until he's behind the bed.

Once there, he moves into the paint of the feature wall behind the bed. He stays there as the Farley's snore, and his partner stays as a window pane. The room remains ultra still as energy from the wall begins to be sent to the Farleys. The colour of the energy was a spacey-purple with starlike twinkles floating around within it.

As this manoeuvred towards the Farleys, something in the background began to move across the moonlight just enough to make the room feel off balance. A spider unknown to Arthur and his partner was originally tucked away at the edge of a curtain. This spider noticed the energy move, which then made Arthur's partner adjust its glimmer through the window straight after.

The spider noticed both things happen. And shot it's webbing at the window whilst moving towards it in the process, whilst growing larger in size. The power of the webbing pushed the window pane out of its frame and towards the floor on the outside of the house.

Arthur's partner and the spider fall out of the window, and crashes are heard soon after  The room has been compromised, the Farleys wake up, and Arthur has to get out of the house as soon as possible!

Arthur shifts himself to the roof of the house into the attic's wooden frames and then shoots onto the thatch of the house. He stands there, and to his utter surprise, he could see a whole street and beyond fighting with one another. People from his academy and others were fighting against Pai's gang.

Everyone involved was changing from creatures to items and everything else in between. Doing whatever they could to outwit the other. Earthquakes were being used, with lava shooting up in the air not long after. The fighting was moving to all streets within Cerne. Some were coming out of portals and then into others.

Arthur didn't know where to start; he shapeshifted into a gargoyle with wings and flew down to where his partner was fighting. He was fighting a monster-sized spider. Arthur flew down and grabbed the spider with his claws and ripped it in half, and tossed its guts away. Arthur's partner jumped onto Arthur's back, and they flew into the air to see what to do next.

Arthur's partner suggests, "We should probably get out of here; it looks like they've been waiting for us."

"What about the others?" Groaned Arthur.

"The item got delivered; that's all we came here to do. My job is to keep you safe and not get you killed, and the same goes for the others. We're partnered up for a reason."

"But we can take them." Arthur started to swoop down towards where more battles were happening. As he did so, Arthur's partner noticed that the button to get sent to the safe place was ingrained into a scale on Arthur's back. He pressed it before Arthur had any ideas of putting their lives in jeopardy.

# *Ten Years Later*

Arthur is sitting on a public bus going to Shirley. He looks out of the window as they travel by a charity shop and a supermarket. Before they get to the end of the road and have to make a turn left, Arthur hears a huge rattling noise coming from within the bus. He looks to the left, and there are three Completely Lardee Dars sitting on the shoulders of each other whilst pushing a food trolley that you would usually associate with being on planes or trains.

Before Arthur had the chance to even ask a question, he was passed a cup of tea on a saucer made with the finest china. After Arthur received the cup of tea, he looked at the Completely Lardee Dars and then took a swig of the drink. Once he swallows it, he's transported to a new location, which consists of being in a massive version of the cup he took a gulp out of.

Arthur is floating in a warm cup of tea which begins to swirl around in a whirlpool motion. Arthur looks up, and he can see himself holding the cup that he's currently in, yet in a trance-type state, then he disappears completely.

Arthur stops looking up and looks to the side of the cup where he's situated. Yet not for long as he continues to swirl around and get pulled in the direction of the middle of the cup. Arthur doesn't particularly struggle against any current; instead, he appears to accept that the whirlpool will take him. Arthur travels to the middle of the whirlpool, where he gets taken and swallowed under.

Moments later, Arthur opens his eyes, and he's sitting in a car outside a bank in Cartoonevenchenso. Shortly after getting to grips with where he is, Arthur looks to the passenger side and a white business card that says 'PLEASE TURN ME OVER' sits there.

Arthur picks it up and turns it over. As he does, three bank robbers run out of the bank holding sacks of cash. Some of the money is flying out of the bags and gliding away as they run towards their red and very obvious getaway vehicle. They manage to get in the car before an overweight and unpassionate security guard comes out of the bank to try and stop them from getting away.

Arthur watches the car drive away and follows it not long after. Arthur drives casually after the getaway car, which is driving frantically from one lane to the other. Scrapping buildings, parked cars, and anything else that is in its proximity at the time. After a couple of minutes, the getaway car drives into a car park of an Italian jazz bar called 'A Steal'. The robbers get out of the car making celebratory noises which sound muffled behind their facemasks.

They grab the sacks of cash, close the door to the car and walk through the front door of the bar. If this was supposed to be a sly bank robbery, it certainly wasn't that.

## Ten Years Ago:

A decade ago, a girl called Saskia fell from the sky. She was propelled in the air from the Cartoonevenchenso train station ticket office. Saskia never intended to arrive at Cartoonevenchenso, and she certainly didn't expect to be falling from such a height with no means to keep her afloat.

Whilst Saskia falls towards a rickety roof, she wonders to herself what it was like to die. She hoped that some of the pleasures she had already experienced in her life would be there in the afterlife. Saskia was keen on peanut butter on toast; she wondered if they would have different types of bread or if it was just one type in the house of death. And Saskia also wondered if toasters were readily available when you die.

As Saskia neared crash landing on a building, she closed her eyes. Saskia just hoped that what was about to happen next wouldn't be too painful. Saskia hit the roof of the building and fell through multiple floors in the process, with debris falling all around until she landed on the ground floor. Saskia lay there in the rubble, motionless as dust bellowed and surrounded the place.

## Amazon Rainforest:

Outside of an ancient tomb which has been deeply covered in the Amazon forest for centuries arrives a tall creature. The creature has its face covered in cloth, only the eyes are revealed. The creature chops away large leaves, branches and tall grass as it tries to clear a path leading to the tomb. After finally reaching the entrance, the creature walks in.

The creature wanders for hours around the tomb, avoiding boobytraps, fighting off ancient warriors, creatures, or just getting lost down the wrong corridor. Until the creature finally found the room that it was looking for.

At the heart of the room that the creature was searching for was a golden statue. Around the statue was nothing but the universe; there was no ceiling, sides or floor. Just twenty-four floating slabs in a row leading to the statue. Each slab was separated by seventy-five centimetres roughly. To get to the statue, you will have to jump to each slab one by one and hope that you don't fall into the abyss of space.

The creature continued without hesitating and jumped from slab to slab all the way to the final slab until the creature was looking at the statue. The statue was of Zikinigh and Kiandria standing up fused to a safe with their hands. One of them was on either side of it. The creature jumped high onto the top of the safe and pulled out a crystal from a pocket. The crystal was called the ongotanunu, and this crystal can only be found in an outer dimension. The creature knocked on the front of the safe with the ongotanunu crystal, and the safe began to radiate light that was even more gold than the gold the safe was made with.

The light radiated around the creature and through the body of it. The slabs began to move, some went clockwise, circulating the statue and the creature, whilst the other slabs went anti-clockwise. The whole of the creature was now completely golden; once it was, it began to levitate above the safe. The clothes began to rip away from the creature; once they had, you could see that it was the Plonkersaurus. Then the safe door opened and the Plonkersaurus was pulled/sucked into the safe. The door closed once the Plonkersaurus was in there, and then the safe ripped itself apart from the hands of Zikinigh and Kiandria. Once completely free of Zikinigh and Kiandria, the safe shot off at lightspeed into the far reaches of space no longer to be seen.

## The End.

ALL RIGHTS RESERVED© 2024

Created by Si Baker ©

Completely Lar Lar Publishing© 2024
This is the property of Si Baker and Completely Lar Lar Publishing© and copyrighted under the UK copyright laws.

The characters in the story are fictional characters and are not based on anyone.

# Dedicated To
Tracey Dominy, Louise Rudkin, George Rudkin, Charlie Rudkin, Alan Rudkin and Rudy Baker.

# In Loving Memory
Tracey Dominy (Mum)
Patricia Ford
Gina Ferguson
Danny Ferguson

Milton Keynes UK
Ingram Content Group UK Ltd.
UKHW032359250824
447288UK00001B/19